DAKOTA
SPRING

YEARLING BOOKS are designed especially to entertain and enlighten young people. Patricia Reilly Giff, consultant to this series, received her bachelor's degree from Marymount College and a master's degree in history from St. John's University. She holds a Professional Diploma in Reading and a Doctorate of Humane Letters from Hofstra University. She was a teacher and reading consultant for many years, and is the author of numerous books for young readers.

DAKOTA SPRING

D. Anne Love

drawings by Ronald Himler

A Yearling Book

Published by
Bantam Doubleday Dell Books for Young Readers
a division of
Bantam Doubleday Dell Publishing Group, Inc.
1540 Broadway
New York, New York 10036

ISBN: 0-440-41290-0

Reprinted by arrangement with Holiday House, Inc.

Printed in the United States of America

March 1997

10   9   8   7   6   5   4

Chapter One

"What do you think she'll be like?" Jess asked. He sat close to the fire, his legs stretched toward the flame. Sonny, our old retriever, whined and turned over, chasing rabbits in his sleep.

"How should I know?" I asked, with more irritation than I meant. Jess is only nine. It's natural he'd be curious about the grandmother we'd never met. I finished chopping the onions and potatoes and dumped them into the stew pot.

Jess snitched a carrot and nibbled on it. "I bet she's got gray hair and thick glasses. And a shawl around her shoulders. I bet she walks like this."

He hunched his shoulders and took a few mincing steps around the kitchen. Sonny raised up and watched for a moment, then went back to his nap.

"It doesn't matter if she's got green hair and two heads," I said. "Pa says we have to be nice to her." I opened the oven door to check on the bread, and the smell of yeast spilled out.

"Are you scared of her, Caroline?" Jess asked.

"No, of course not. Go see if Pa needs anything. Tell him supper's almost ready."

Jess's boots made a hollow sound on the wooden floor. He opened the door to Pa's room and closed it again. I wiped my hands on my apron and went to the window.

Outside, the last weak rays of sun cast long shadows across the prairie. The dirt road leading away from our farm stretched like a brown ribbon toward the horizon. It seemed that the road never brought us anything but sorrow. I stood remembering the day the doctor came to tell us Mama had died and wouldn't be coming home again. Then, just last week, he'd made the trip again, this time with Pa lying on a pile of blankets in the back of the wagon, limp as my old rag doll.

Pa had fallen while helping Mr. McGuffey put up a new barn. Now he lay in the room he'd shared with Mama, one leg broken, his shattered ribs held together with tight bandages, his face a mass of bruises turning from deep purple to a sickly yellow. It would be months before he could work again. Mr. McGuffey and our other neighbors would help with spring planting, but there was no one but Jess to help me look after Pa and do the chores.

"I'll stay home from school this term, Pa," I'd said, when Pa was finally able to talk. "Jess and I can manage till you're well."

But Pa wouldn't hear of it. He was determined that Jess and I wouldn't miss another day of school. So he sent word to our grandmother all the way to Charleston, South Carolina. And now she was coming to take care of two grandchildren she'd never even met.

Her letter lay on the table where Pa had left it. I turned from the window and picked it up.

Dear James,

I'm sure I don't have to tell you how unhappy I am at the prospect of traveling all the way to Dakota to care for your children. Especially at this time of year

[4]

when I have so many obligations here in Charleston. I warned Rebecca that no good could ever come from marrying you and living at the edge of civilization, but she always was headstrong. However, there's no point in speaking unkindly of the dead, is there?

I will stay for one month. I shall expect your children to conduct themselves properly, as I cannot tolerate unruly behavior. I shall come by train, arriving on the 25th of March. I trust you will at least send someone to meet me.

Yours,
Abigail Ravenell

"Abigail," I said aloud. "Grandmother Abigail. Grandmother Ravenell."

"What are you muttering about?" Jess asked, coming back into the kitchen. "Pa says to tell you he's starved."

"Supper's almost ready." I folded our grandmother's letter and put it back on the table.

Jess glanced at the envelope with its spidery writing. "Do you think she'll like us, Caroline?" He looked as uncertain as I felt. Judging from her letter, it didn't seem likely. But there was no point in worrying Jess.

"I'm sure she will once she gets to know us," I said. I handed him a stack of bowls and three spoons. "Here. Set the table for me, and then we'll go get Pa."

When supper was on the table, Jess and I went into Pa's room and helped him out of bed. He put his arms around our shoulders and we shuffled to the kitchen. I dragged his chair up to the table and stuffed it with pillows to cushion him.

Night had come down, and I lit the oil lamp before we sat down. Sonny woke up and wagged his tail, then sat by Pa's chair.

Pa said, "You rascal! Do you think I'm going to share this delicious stew with you?"

Sonny licked his chops and we all laughed. Pa tasted the soup. "This is excellent, honey," he said to me. "Your grandmother will be surprised to see what a fine cook you are."

"Pa, what should we call her?" I asked. "Grandmother Abigail? Grandmother Ravenell?"

Pa spread some butter on his bread. "Why don't you ask her what she'd prefer?"

"Will she like us, Pa?" Jess asked.

"Well now," Pa said. "I expect she will after she's been here awhile. Remember, son, it'll take her some time to get used to us. And Dakota's very different from Charleston."

"Have you ever been there, Pa?"

"Once. Many years ago. I met your mother there." Suddenly Pa seemed to be a million miles away. "I remember she wore a blue dress and white flowers in her hair. Prettiest girl I'd ever seen."

Jess picked up his bowl and drank his last bit of soup.

"Jess!" Pa thundered. "Don't do that! Mind your manners!"

"Sorry, Pa." Jess looked at me, his eyes brimming with tears. I winked at him.

"Let's practice our company manners," I suggested.

"Okay." Jess sniffed loudly and wiped his nose on the back of his sleeve. I sighed.

"Please pass the soup," Jess said.

I spooned more soup into his bowl. "Now wait for it to cool," I coached. "And don't slurp."

Jess slipped Sonny a bite of bread and drummed his fingers on the table, peering into his bowl as if staring at his soup would make it cool faster. He looked up. "Hey, Caroline. Watch. Guess what this is."

He drew a deep breath, crossed his eyes, and sucked in his cheeks until his mouth practically disappeared. He moved his lips in and out like a fish looking for food.

A smile stole across Pa's face, but he said, "Don't make faces at the table, son."

Jess let his breath out in a loud whoosh and stirred his soup. He grinned at me. "I can make my eyeballs disappear. Want to see?"

"No, she doesn't," Pa answered. "You're supposed to be practicing your best manners, remember?"

In the flickering lamplight, Pa's eyes met mine across the table. I decided to teach by example. "Tell us about Charleston, Pa," I said, in my most polite, table-conversation voice.

"Mind you, it's been a long while since I was there," Pa said. "But as I recollect, it's a right beautiful place. They have palmetto trees, and big fancy houses in all the colors of the rainbow, and cobblestone streets that stretch all the way down to the water."

Pa took a long sip of his coffee. "Your grandmother's house is so close to the harbor that the Union soldiers shelled it during the war."

"The soldiers shot at her house?" Jess asked, his eyes wide.

"Yes, indeed. In fact, to this very day, there's a cannonball still stuck in the roof."

"Was our grandmother afraid?"

Pa laughed and ruffled Jess's hair. "Your grandmother Ravenell is not afraid of the devil himself. Now, finish your soup, please, and help me back to bed. These old bones are aching pretty bad."

We finished eating, and Jess and I helped Pa back to bed. After we washed and dried the dishes, Jess took Sonny outside and I sat down with my school books. But it was impossible to concentrate on verbs and nouns and fractions. Like Jess, I wondered what our grandmother would be like, and whether she would like us, even a little bit.

Chapter Two

When March 25 rolled around, Pa sent me
with Mr. McGuffey to fetch our grandmother from the train. Jess begged to go,
too, but Pa needed his help at home.

Mr. McGuffey came for me just before
sunrise. The morning was cold and clear
when we set out on the road toward town.
Mr. McGuffey didn't talk much, except to

the horses. They plodded along, kicking up a cloud of dust that swirled and drifted in the wind.

The blue-eyed grass waved in the breeze, and the Indian paintbrush made splashes of dull orange amid the patches of blue-tinged snow still lying in the shady places. A prairie thrush darted across the road and hid herself in the tall grasses.

The sun rose, warming our faces. Mr. McGuffey lit his pipe and the smoke curled over his shoulders. A gopher poked its head from its hole beside the road and scurried away again.

"Humphh," said Mr. McGuffey. "Did you see that gopher?"

"Yes, sir."

"Know what it means when you see one this early?"

"No, sir."

"Means we're going to have a stormy spring. Sure as shootin'. Tell your pa I'll be over to do his planting soon as I can. Ought to get everything in the ground before the rains hit."

"I'll tell him," I said.

We heard the train's bell clanging as we rumbled into the station. Suddenly my mouth went dry and my chest felt tight. I had no idea what my grandmother looked like. How would I recognize her?

We watched the passengers come down the steps from the platform. First came two women with babies in their arms, and then two older ladies carrying matching leather suitcases. A farmer in tattered wool pants came next, then a young man wearing wire-rimmed glasses and an overcoat.

"Well," said Mr. McGuffey. "Which one is your grandmother?"

I scanned the empty platform. My throat closed up, and I felt tears sting my eyes. "I guess she didn't come after all," I said. "How could she do this? Pa was counting on her!"

"Could be she missed her train somewhere along the way," said Mr. McGuffey. He patted my shoulder. "Don't you worry now, I'll just go talk to the stationmaster. Maybe we can figure out what happened."

Just then we heard a commotion and turned back to the platform. The stationmaster struggled down the steps carrying two large trunks. Behind him strode a woman in a gray suit, black leather boots, and a feathered hat.

"For heaven's sake, young man, do be careful!" she said to the stationmaster. "That's a matched set of trunks you're carrying, not sacks of cattle feed!"

She stopped on the bottom step and looked around. The moment her gaze met mine, I felt a thrill crawl up my spine. I'd looked into those same black eyes before. They were my mother's eyes.

I went to where she stood, my heart hammering in my chest. Mr. McGuffey followed.

"Mrs. Abigail Ravenell?" I asked.

"Yes?" One of her eyebrows went up and she stared at me until I felt my face turn hot.

"I'm Caroline. Your granddaughter."

"Hmm. I might have known. Stop blushing, girl. Your mother had that same annoying habit. It's a sign of weakness in one's character, I always say."

I stood speechless. Mr. McGuffey introduced himself and said, "We've come to take you home, Miz Ravenell."

"Home, Mr. McGuffey, is in Charleston. I can't imagine ever living in such a desolate place as this." She shook her head. "A hundred miles from anywhere. I don't see how my daughter stood it as long as she did, God rest her soul."

Mr. McGuffey's eyebrows went up but he didn't say anything. He loaded my grandmother's trunks onto the wagon and helped her onto the seat. I sat behind them on a blanket, and we turned the wagon for home.

I studied the back of my grandmother's head. She was nothing like I had imagined. A mass of dark curls peeked from beneath her feathered hat. She had a graceful neck and tiny ears as perfect as those on a porcelain doll. When she turned her head, I saw that her nose was small and straight, her chin strong, and her eyelashes dark and feathery against her pale skin.

"Don't stare, Caroline," she said. "It's impolite."

I jumped. How could she know I'd been watching her?

"Look," said Mr. McGuffey at last. "There's your farm."

I squinted into the setting sun. The house and the barn were dark specks on the horizon. We clattered past the fenced fields, past the poplar trees Mama planted the year Jess was born. When we stopped in the dusty yard, Sonny came from under the porch, barking. The windmill creaked in the wind, making patterns of light, then dark, on the ground. A figure appeared in the doorway, then darted away again. A moment later, Jess burst through the door and down the steps.

"I'm Jess," he announced. "And you're my grandmother."

"So it seems." Grandmother Abigail placed one gloved hand in Mr. McGuffey's roughened one and waited for him to help her down off the wagon. She brushed the dust from her sleeves and peered at Jess as if he had come from another planet.

"What on earth happened to your hair?" she asked.

It was then I noticed that Jess's hair looked as if it had been chewed up in Pa's plow.

Tears welled in my brother's eyes. "I wanted to make a good impression," he said. "I gave myself a haircut."

"With what, pinking shears?"

Jess's bottom lip trembled and a single tear

spilled down his cheek. I looked at my grand-mother through a red haze. Couldn't she see how hard he was trying to please her? He was just a little boy. Why did she have to be so hard on him?

Mr. McGuffey cleared his throat. "I'll just take these trunks in for you, Miz Ravenell," he said. He picked them up and disappeared into the house.

I put my arm around Jess. "Don't worry about your hair," I whispered. "After sup-per, I'll help you even it up."

Jess sniffed and wiped his face on his sleeve. We followed our grandmother into the house.

Chapter Three

We put Grandmother in Pa's room. It had a feather bed with a brass headboard and a pine washstand Pa bought in Chicago. I'd put the quilt that had been our mother's on the bed, and Jess filled a bottle with blue-eyed grass.

Grandmother ran her fingers over the quilt. Her eyes held a faraway look.

"It was our mother's," I said.

"Yes, I know. I helped her make it." For the first time since getting off the train, our grandmother seemed almost human. Then she got all brisk and businesslike again.

"Well, if you children will excuse me, I'd like to unpack before dinner."

We made a bed for Pa on the floor in the kitchen, next to the fireplace. Jess and I made our beds on pallets in the loft. I lit the lamp for Pa, and he opened his Bible and put on his spectacles. I sliced a ham, started the potatoes, and cut the apple pie Mr. McGuffey's wife had sent.

After a while, Grandmother appeared. She had changed from her gray suit into a plain blue dress. "What are you reading, James?" she asked.

"The Bible, Abigail. You ought to try it sometime," Pa said. I couldn't tell if he was joking or not.

"Don't be impertinent," Grandmother

said. To me she said, "Where's your teapot? I could do with a cup."

I put the kettle on and took Mama's blue-and-white teapot from the cupboard. I sliced some bread, set the table, and dragged Pa's chair into place. Grandmother sat quietly, watching me.

It made me nervous. Then it made me angry. I thought she'd come to help me. Instead, she was sitting there like the queen of Sheba and being hateful to Jess because of his haircut.

My head jerked up. Where *was* Jess? I hadn't seen him in over an hour.

"Pa, where's Jess?"

"Hmmm?" Pa looked up from his reading. "Oh, I'm sure he's around somewhere. Go find Sonny and you'll find Jess. He and that dog are always together."

I went out to the porch. The wind had come up. It smelled like rain. "Jess! Sonny! Supper!" I yelled.

There was no answer. "Jess? Where are you?"

I heard a thumping sound and then Jess's loud "Shhhh!"

I looked down and saw a flash of blue shirt and brown dog as Jess and Sonny huddled beneath the porch. I dropped to my stomach and put my eye to the cracks between the planks. "Jess! What are you doing under there?"

"I'm going to live here forever and ever. Just me and Sonny. And I'm not coming out till she's gone!"

"It's going to get awful cold and wet under there. Can't you smell the rain in the air?"

"I don't care," Jess said. "I'd rather drown than be around that mean old witch."

"Don't let Pa hear you say that," I warned. "He said we have to be nice to her no matter what."

"How come we have to be nice to her but she gets to say mean things to us?"

It was a good question. "She doesn't mean

to hurt our feelings," I said. "It's been a long time since she's been around anybody our age. I guess it'll take her some time to get used to us."

"I don't care. She's hateful and I hate her and I'm not going to be her grandson. Not ever."

"Well then, could you just pretend to be her grandson? Just for the next month? Till Pa's better?"

"I don't know," Jess said. "A month is a long time."

"It's not so long," I said. "By the time school is out, she'll be gone. We'll go swimming in the creek every day, and pick wild blackberries, and build that fort you wanted. Remember?"

I heard a scooting sound and Jess's head appeared. "Really? You'd help me build a fort?"

"If you'll help me while our grandmother's here."

"Deal. Come on, Sonny."

They came from beneath the porch, Sonny's tail filmed with cobwebs and Jess covered with so much dirt I could have planted potatoes in his ears. "You can't let her see you like that," I said.

Jess brushed himself off, sending clouds of dust mushrooming around him. "You're right," he said. "It wouldn't make a very good impression."

We laughed out loud then, and Pa's voice drifted out to us. "Jess? Caroline? Are you coming to supper?"

"Go around back," I told Jess. "I'll bring you a clean shirt. Be sure you wash up good before she sees you. And hurry!"

He did. Ten minutes later, we were all seated at the table. Pa, Jess, Grandmother, and me. We held hands and Pa said a blessing.

"For all these thy gifts, O Lord, we are truly grateful."

And please help Jess remember his manners, I added silently.

Pa passed the ham and potatoes to our grandmother, then to me and Jess. When our plates were full, he said, "Well, Jess, what have you learned in school this week?"

Jess shrugged and took a bite of ham.

"Oh, come now," our grandmother said. "Surely you remember *something* you learned. What about arithmetic? What did you work on today?"

"I didn't go to school today," Jess told her. "I had to stay home to take care of Pa."

Grandmother waved her fork impatiently. "Yesterday, then."

Jess swallowed. "Subtraction."

"That's better," she said, nodding. "What's ten minus six?"

"Four."

"Eight minus two?"

"Six. May I have some dessert now?" Jess shot me a helpless look.

"In a minute," I said. "As soon as everyone else has finished."

"What about your studies, Caroline?" our grandmother asked.

"We're studying geometry. And poetry."

"How lovely. Logic on the one hand and emotion on the other. More ham, James?"

"I know a poem," Jess put in. "Want to hear it?"

Oh no. I knew what was coming. Jess and his best friend, Lucas, had been reciting the same disgusting verse for weeks. It wasn't exactly the kind of poem a grandmother would appreciate. Especially at the supper table. My foot shot out, seeking Jess's under the table.

"Ow!" our grandmother cried, shifting in her chair.

My face flamed. "I'm sorry," I muttered, wishing the floor would open up and swallow me.

"Here's my poem," Jess went on. "It's really funny."

I tried desperately to catch Pa's eye, but

he turned to Jess as if he expected a sonnet like the ones Mama used to read aloud on winter afternoons. Jess began:

"A hungry hunter took an ax
And gave a rabbit forty whacks.
And when he saw what he could do,
He made the guts into a stew,
And gave the next one forty-two!"

Our grandmother stopped chewing. Her fork clattered onto her plate.

Jess gave her an angelic smile. "Funny, huh?"

Pa said, "That'll do, Jess. You're excused."

"But Pa, I haven't had dessert yet!"

Pa pointed his spoon at Jess. "And there won't *be* any until you learn to mind your manners at the table. Apologize to your grandmother."

"Sorry," Jess mumbled. His chair scraped on the floor when he stood up.

Pa said to our grandmother, "I'm sorry too, Abigail. Would you like some more coffee?"

"No thank you, James. I should give Caroline a hand with these dishes. If I'm to be of use around here, I might as well get started."

We got Pa settled before the fire, and I showed her where I kept the pots and pans and how we heated water from the well to wash them. I showed her how to make a fire in the potbellied stove, and pointed out the cupboard where I kept flour, salt, sugar, and spices.

"Well," she said, "it's every bit as primitive as I'd imagined. But there's nothing to be done about it, is there? What time shall I wake you in the morning? Six? Seven?"

Pa laughed out loud. "Seven? Boy, do you have a lot to learn, Abigail. These children are up at four, winter and summer."

She looked horrified. "Four? A.M.?"

"Yes, ma'am," Jess said. He had stolen back into the room. Now he sat in the corner with Sonny. He ticked off our chores on his fingers. "We milk the cow, clean the stalls, and put down fresh hay. Then we feed the sheep, bring in wood for the fire, and draw water from the well."

"You do all that?" Our grandmother seemed genuinely amazed.

Jess nodded. "Uh-huh. Then we have breakfast and go to school."

Pa reached up and squeezed my hand. "They're hard workers, Abigail. I couldn't do without them."

"I can see that," our grandmother said. "Well. I had no idea."

"Don't worry," Pa said to her. "I'm not expecting you to muck out the sheep pens or haul wood. If you'll just keep the household running and look after Jess, Caroline and Mr. McGuffey will handle the rest till I'm on my feet again."

Grandmother looked enormously relieved. "Well," she said again. "Yes, James. I believe I can do that. But I must be back in Charleston by the end of April."

"I understand."

"Well, then, if you all will excuse me, I think I'll go to bed. I've had a long journey and I'm tired."

"Of course," Pa said. "We're most grateful to you for coming, Abigail."

Jess said, "Wait! What should we call you? Pa said we should ask."

"I beg your pardon?"

"Should we call you Grandmother, or Grandmother Abigail, or Grandmother Ravenell?" Jess asked. "Or should we call you just plain Abigail, like Pa does?"

A tiny frown creased her smooth forehead. "Certainly not! Children don't address adults by their given names."

"May we call you Grandmother Abigail?" I asked.

She sighed, and her dark eyes darted, birdlike, between Jess and me. Then she said, "I believe I'd feel more comfortable if you called me Mrs. Ravenell."

"But . . . ," Jess began.

Pa stopped him with a frown and a shake of his head. "If that's what you prefer, then Mrs. Ravenell it is. Say good night, children."

"Good night," Jess murmured.

"Good night," I said. I just couldn't bring myself to call her Mrs. Ravenell. It sounded so formal. As if she were a stranger Pa had hired to help out instead of our own flesh and blood.

When the door to her room closed, Jess threw himself into my arms. "She hates us!" he sobbed. "She doesn't even want to be our grandmother. I wish she'd never come here. I wish she'd get on the train and go back home tomorrow."

Pa looked pained. He sat up a little straighter on his bed of pillows and drew us down beside him. "Maybe I should never have sent for her," he said quietly. "I just didn't know what else to do."

"It's all right, Pa," I said. "We can stand anything for a month. Can't we, Jess?"

Jess shrugged. "I guess. But it's going to be a long month."

"That's my boy," Pa said. "And when I'm well again, we'll do something special to celebrate."

He kissed us both and said, "Go to sleep now. Tomorrow is a school day."

Jess and I climbed the ladder to the loft. Jess fell asleep right away, but I lay wide awake, listening to the night sounds. Through the crack in the roof, I could see a single star winking in the blue-black sky. I remembered Mama, her voice rich and low, teaching me the old nursery rhyme. *Star light, star bright, I wish I may, I wish I might, have the wish I wish tonight.*

I made a wish. Three wishes. I wished for Pa to get well soon. I wished that our grandmother would like Jess and me. And I wished we didn't have to call her Mrs. Ravenell.

Chapter Four

The next day, when Jess and I came up the road from school, we saw Pa on the front porch, leaning on a pair of crutches. We broke into a run. It was a relief to see Pa looking normal again.

"Pa!" Jess yelled. "You're good as new!"

Pa laughed. "Not quite, son, but I'm working on it."

He tapped his crutches. "Mr. McGuffey brought these from town. It sure feels good to be standing upright."

"Well, don't overdo it," said our grandmother from the doorway. "It wouldn't do to fall and break those bones all over again."

Jess opened his geography book and took out a sheet of paper. He unfolded it and gave it to our grandmother. "Mrs. Ravenell, I drew this for you in school today."

She took the paper from Jess, surprise showing on her face. "Why, thank you, Jess. It's very nice."

"It's a picture of the house and the windmill. So you won't forget us when you go back to Charleston."

For a moment, the two of them just looked at each other. Finally, Mrs. Ravenell folded the paper and put it in her apron pocket. Then she said, "Come in now and change your clothes. I need wood and water before I can cook supper."

We went inside. Jess and I changed clothes and started our chores. By the time we got back with firewood and water, Mrs. Ravenell had a pie ready for the oven. Pa sat at the table drawing on a sheet of paper.

"Are you making a picture for Mrs. Ravenell, too?" Jess asked, dropping his load of logs on the hearth.

"No, I'm making a sketch for Mr. McGuffey so he'll know where to plant our seeds. He's coming on Saturday and he'll need your help."

"Oh, Pa. Me and Lucas were planning to go fishing. Wouldn't you like to have a nice fresh trout for supper?"

Pa grinned at him. "Sure would. But I'd rather have our crops planted so we'll have plenty to eat and plenty for the sheep come next winter. I'm counting on you, son."

Mrs. Ravenell started the fire in the cookstove and filled the teakettle. "I'm sure he won't let you down, James. Will you, Jess?"

Jess bit his lip. "No, ma'am."

"Good. That's settled. And Caroline."

"Yes, ma'am?"

"Mrs. McGuffey came by today. She tells me your teacher has chosen you to recite your poem at the Founder's Day celebration next month."

I felt my face turn red. I hadn't told anybody about that.

"Well, speak up, girl. Were you chosen or weren't you?"

"Yes, Mrs. Ravenell."

Pa's face was wreathed in smiles. "Honey, that's wonderful! Why didn't you tell us?"

I shrugged. "I don't have a decent dress to wear, Pa. Besides, since you got hurt, I've had more important things to worry about."

The minute I said it, I wished I could take it all back. The light went out of Pa's eyes. I could tell he was wishing Mama were alive. She would know what to do about a daughter whose arms and legs suddenly seemed too long for any of her clothes.

I went to the table and put my arms around Pa's neck. "It's not important," I said. "Besides, you know me. I turn red and get tongue-tied when I have to talk in front of people."

"All the more reason you should do it," Mrs. Ravenell interjected, wiping her hands on her apron. She lit the oil lamp and set it on the table. Shadows danced against the walls. "The only way to overcome one's shortcomings is to face them. Isn't that so, James?"

"Well now—" Pa began.

"What's a shortcoming?" Jess asked. "When can we eat? I'm hungry."

"Don't interrupt," Mrs. Ravenell said. "It's impolite. Go wash your hands and help your sister set the table."

I was glad there was no more talk about me and the Founder's Day poem. During supper, we talked about the crops and the new lambs that would be born in April.

The rest of the week flew by. On Saturday, Mr. McGuffey and several of our neighbors came to the house. They drank coffee with Pa and studied the sketch he'd drawn. Then Jess and I went with them to the fields. We started at sunup and finished just before dark. When we got back to the house, Pa thanked the men for their help.

"It's the least I could do," Mr. McGuffey said. "If you hadn't been helping me with my barn, you wouldn't have been hurt. But I don't mind telling you, I'm glad to have the planting done, James. It's going to be a stormy spring."

"How can you be so sure, Mr. McGuffey?" Mrs. Ravenell asked. "Surely no one can predict weather so far into the future."

Mr. McGuffey smiled. "I can feel it in these old bones, Miz Ravenell. They hardly ever lie. You mark my words. We're in for a real blow before summer rolls around."

Pa said, "Let's hope it holds off till those seeds have taken root."

"Yes, indeed," said Mr. McGuffey. "Well, we'd best be getting home. Supper's waiting."

We went out with them to their wagons and watched till they disappeared around the bend. Pa leaned against his crutches and scanned the neat rows that seemed to stretch forever toward the darkening horizon. Streaks of pink and gold lit the sky, and the air smelled of damp earth. In their pens, the sheep shuffled and bleated, and the windmill spun slowly in the breeze.

"Would you look at that," Pa said, his voice soft. "If there's a finer sight in the whole world, I don't know what it is."

Just then, Jess rounded the barn, Sonny at his heels. "Hey, Pa!" he yelled. "Hey, Caroline! Watch! Watch what Sonny can do!"

He made Sonny sit on his haunches. He lifted the dog's front legs and held them high in the air. "Beg, Sonny!" he commanded. "Come on, boy. Beg!"

He let go of Sonny, and the dog flopped into the dirt, graceless as a sack of potatoes.

Jess looked stricken. "He did it just a minute ago. Honest!"

He bent over to haul Sonny to his feet again, but Sonny saw what was coming. He rolled over onto his back and waved his legs in the air.

"Come on, Sonny," Jess coaxed. "Show 'em you know how to beg, boy."

Sonny's tongue lolled to one side and he eyed Jess warily.

Jess looked up at Pa and me. "I guess he needs some more practice."

Pa chuckled. "Don't be too hard on him, son. You know what they say. You can't teach an old dog new tricks."

Jess dropped to his knees in the dirt and scratched Sonny's pink belly. "He's not *that* old. He can learn. He's a lot smarter than a orda-nary dog."

Behind us, the door creaked open. "Supper's waiting, everyone," Mrs. Ravenell said. We went in.

We didn't go to church the next day. After breakfast, Pa read to us from the Bible, and then Jess whistled for Sonny and went off to play. It was a perfect Dakota spring day, cool and sunny. I helped Mrs. Ravenell wash the dishes and make the beds, and then took one of Mama's books out to the porch.

I was halfway through it when Mrs. Ravenell called, "Caroline? Would you come here, please?"

I found her standing in her room. On the bed was a pile of the most beautiful dresses I'd ever seen. Green silk, pink cotton, gray wool, spilled across the bed like a handful of jewels.

"There should be something here we can alter to fit you," my grandmother said. "I want you to recite your poem at the Founder's Day picnic."

"Oh!" I could only stare at the beautiful clothes.

"Close your mouth, Caroline. You look as if you're catching flies."

"But, Mrs. Ravenell, these are all so pretty. Are you sure you want to cut them up to fit me?"

"Quite sure." She picked up a green dress with a matching jacket and held it against me, considering.

"Yes, indeed," she said finally. "I believe this will do quite nicely. Have you any thread?"

My heart sank. "None this color."

"Well, never mind. I'm sure we can find some in town. We shall ask Mrs. McGuffey to bring it on her next trip."

"Oh, Grand . . . Mrs. Ravenell! I've never had anything so beautiful. Thank you, thank you!"

"You're quite welcome. And don't gush, Caroline. It's unbecoming. A simple expression of gratitude is sufficient. Now. I wonder if I might hear this poem of yours."

I took a deep breath and recited it for her. I only forgot a couple of words. When I finished, she nodded and said, "Very nice. Your teacher made a wise choice. Now, if you don't mind, I'd like a nap."

Pa was asleep on his pallet on the floor. I was too excited about the dress to go back to my book, so I went down the road, under the fence, and around the bend to the creek that ran along one edge of our farm. The last of the ice had melted and the water tumbled freely over moss-covered rocks. The wild blackberry bushes had leafed out. When summer came, there would be plenty of fruit for Pa's favorite cobbler.

"Hey! Hey, Caroline! Come here." It was Jess.

I hurried toward the sound of his voice

and found him and Sonny at the entrance to a cave on the creek bank.

"Look what we found! A real robbers' cave!"

I peered in. The cave was barely big enough for one person. "Must have been a baby robber," I said.

"Oh, Caroline!" Jess grinned. "This would make a good hideout," he said. "I'm going to get Pa's shovel and make it bigger. Will you help me?"

"I don't know, Jess. It might not be safe. What if the top caved in on you?"

"It won't. I'm going to put some branches in the dirt to make the roof stronger. When I'm done, me and Sonny will have a secret hideout. Please, Caroline?"

"All right. But we have to hurry. Pa wants us to clean out the sheep pens this afternoon."

"On Sunday?" Jess looked pained.

"On Sunday. Come on."

We took the shortcut across the field and got Pa's shovel from the barn. Jess took the hatchet and cut some branches for the roof. I got down on my knees at the entrance to the cave and started digging. Inside the cave the air smelled dank. The dirt was wet and heavy, and after an hour my arms ached.

"Hey!" Jess said when he saw what I'd done. "This is perfect, Caroline! Here, help me with the roof."

We wedged the branches into the wet earth and smoothed mud on top. Then we shoveled out the dirt and put down some branches for a floor. We crawled inside with Sonny between us. It was a tight fit, but Jess was delighted.

"Guess what I'm going to do?" he crowed. "I'm going to bring some candles, and a blanket, and some food, and camp out down here all night. Just me and Sonny."

"What about me? I'm the one who did all the work. Sonny didn't help at all."

Jess giggled. "A dog can't use a shovel."

"Well, that's not my problem." I tried not to smile, but Jess saw that I was teasing him. He put one arm around my shoulder and grinned. "Aw, Caroline!"

"Come on," I said. "We'd better put these tools up and get to those sheep pens."

We took the shovel and the hatchet and cut across the field once again. Sonny lumbered along between us, a stick in his mouth. Mrs. Ravenell waited for us on the front porch.

When she saw us, her hands flew to her face. "Oh, my heavens! What on earth happened to you?"

That was when I noticed that Jess and I were something of a mess. Mud clung to our hair, our hands, our clothes, our shoes. And Sonny looked like a mud pie with legs.

"We built a hideout," Jess explained. "In a cave."

"More like a pigsty, I'd say." I could tell

Mrs. Ravenell was furious. She clenched her hands so tightly that her knuckles turned white, and her lips made a thin, tight line.

"I came all the way out here to try to help you children out, and while I'm doing everything in my power to bring you up decently, you do everything possible to disgrace yourselves! What I'm going to do with you, I'm sure I don't know."

She glared at me. "And after I've already ripped that dress apart to make it over for you."

"I'm sorry," I said. "I was just helping Jess. We didn't mean to get so dirty."

Mrs. Ravenell shook her head. "Just look at you! What must I do to persuade you to act like civilized human beings? *Beg?*"

Right then, Sonny plopped down in front of her and raised his filthy front paws high in the air.

Jess, the human mud ball, went crazy. "Caroline, look! He's begging! Just like I taught him." He danced around the yard. "I told you he could do it! I told you he was smarter than a orda-nary dog!"

Pa thumped to the porch on his crutches. "What's the trouble, Abigail?"

"See for yourself," Mrs. Ravenell said.

Pa looked down at the two of us, and at Sonny, lying at Jess's feet. The corners of his mouth twitched into the beginnings of a smile. But he said sternly, "You both know better than to wallow in the mud. Go wash yourselves at the well, and then get out of those clothes. There'll be no supper for either of you tonight."

Mrs. Ravenell nodded. I guess she felt satisfied.

Jess and I took turns pouring buckets of water over each other's heads. When we were clean, we left our shoes on the back porch and changed our clothes. We spent the rest of the afternoon cleaning the sheep pens and putting down fresh hay. We waited till

Mrs. Ravenell had gone to her room for the night before we went inside.

Pa sat at the table, drinking coffee. He grinned and put a finger to his lips when we came in. "Are you hungry?" he whispered.

I shook my head, but Jess whispered back, "I'm starved!"

Pa opened a napkin he'd hidden on his lap. Inside were two thick slices of bread, still warm from the oven, and smeared with strawberry jam. My mouth watered. Suddenly I was famished.

We each took a piece. Pa said, in a real low voice, "Usually I don't hold with deceiving people, but I know you didn't mean to do anything wrong today."

"We were just having fun," Jess said between bites.

"I know that," Pa said. "But you have to remember, your grandmother isn't used to being around children. I want you both to promise me you'll try harder from now on not to upset her."

"We promise," we said together.

"Good," Pa said. "Now, you'd better get to bed. And remember, not a word about this to your grandmother."

He kissed us and we scrambled up the ladder to the loft. Jess said, "Do you think Mrs. Ravenell is really, really mad?"

"I think she was until Pa punished us."

"Maybe we should do something to show her how sorry we are," Jess said.

I pulled the covers up to my chin. "Like what?"

"I don't know. Just something."

"I'll think about it," I said. "Go to sleep."

"Okay. Caroline?"

"What?"

"Thanks for helping me with the hideout."

"You're welcome."

"Caroline?"

I sighed. "*What*, Jess?"

"You can hide out with me anytime you want."

"Thanks," I said. "I appreciate that."

A few minutes later, Jess lay snoring quietly. I thought about what he'd said. Maybe we should find some way to apologize to Mrs. Ravenell. I thought about it for a long time and finally hatched a plan.

In the morning, I woke Jess an hour earlier than usual. We dressed in the dark and climbed down from the loft in our stocking feet. We tiptoed past Pa, asleep on the floor, and carried our shoes and coats outside. The door creaked once when we closed it.

Our breath came out in clouds. The dark sky shimmered with stars. We put on our coats and shoes, and I filled Jess in on the plan.

"We'll get all the chores done and then make a special breakfast for Pa and Mrs. Ravenell. By the time she gets up, thinking she has to make tea and fry the bacon and make biscuits, it'll all be done."

"Good idea, Caroline!" Jess thumped me on the shoulder. "That should put her in a good mood."

We went out to the sheep. They shuffled and bleated in their pens, and Jess tiptoed around them, saying "Shhhh!" as if they understood him. By the time we fed them and carried firewood to the house, the sky had lightened a little. We saw a lamp flicker on in the kitchen, and then a wisp of gray smoke curled from the chimney.

"Pa's awake," Jess said, his voice low.

We went in, and Pa blinked at us. "Did I oversleep?"

I shook my head and explained our plan.

"Your morning chores are already done?" Pa whispered.

We nodded. I said, "I'm going to start breakfast now."

Pa hugged me. "Your mama would sure be proud of you."

"What about me?" Jess asked.

"You too, son."

Jess beamed.

I tied on my apron and shoved wood into the cookstove. "Well, don't just stand there," I murmured to Jess.

He went to the cupboard and took down Mama's lace tablecloth, her best white china plates, and her blue-and-white teapot. While he tiptoed around, setting the table, I got the biscuits ready for the oven, fried the bacon, and put the teakettle on. Pretty soon, the house smelled like morning.

The door to Mrs. Ravenell's room flew open, and she stood there, her hair a tumble of unruly curls, her bare toes peeking from beneath the ruffled hem of her dressing gown. "What in the . . ."

"Surprise!" Jess yelled. "We made breakfast. Just for you."

Mrs. Ravenell looked startled. "Well, I appreciate the gesture, but what about your chores? Won't you be late for school?"

"All done," Jess informed her. "We got up early. Extra, extra early."

"So it would seem." She waved her hand toward the lace tablecloth, the white china. "What's all this?"

"Mama used it for company," I said. "Jess and I wanted to make a special breakfast for you. We're truly sorry about yesterday."

"Here, Mrs. Ravenell, sit right down." Jess held her chair as if he were a waiter in a fine restaurant.

"But I'm not dressed!" she protested, raking her hair away from her face.

Pa said, "Don't stand on ceremony, Abigail. We're family. I don't reckon the world will end if you eat breakfast this one time without your shoes."

"Well. . . ." She smoothed the ribbons on her dressing gown.

"Come on, Mrs. Ravenell," Jess urged. "You don't want your biscuits to get cold."

I poured the tea and took the biscuits out

of the oven. Jess helped Pa into his chair and we all sat down.

Mrs. Ravenell studied us over the rim of her cup.

Jess and I waited. Finally she said, "It was wrong of you to wallow in the mud like barnyard animals, but perhaps I scolded you a bit too harshly."

Jess elbowed me under the table.

"They're good children, Abigail," Pa said. "They work as hard as any grown farmhand. I guess we shouldn't be too hard on them if they forget themselves and act like children now and then."

"I realize that, James. I've already admitted my error. I should like it very much if this episode were never mentioned again."

"Does that mean you're not mad anymore?" Jess asked.

Her eyebrows went up. She stirred more milk into her tea. Then she said, "You're forgiven, this time. But don't think for one minute that gives you permission to continue behaving like wild animals. Now, finish your breakfast."

She poured more tea for Pa. "And Caroline. You will please come straight home this afternoon. We should work on fitting your dress for Founder's Day."

She made her voice sound stern, but just for a moment, her black eyes twinkled. A smile so small I thought at first I'd imagined it flitted across her lips. But Jess saw it, too. He grinned and gave me another poke in the ribs.

Chapter Five

"Let's see now, who hasn't answered a question today?" Miss Simpson stood in front of the blackboard, her blue gaze sweeping over us. I glanced across the schoolroom to where Jess sat with Lucas and the other nine-year-olds. Jess stopped making his fish faces at Lucas and slid a little farther down in his seat. I knew what he was thinking. *Please, Miss Simpson, don't call on me.*

So of course she did. "Jess, would you please stand and name the seven continents."

He took so long getting out of his seat that I thought Christmas might actually come first. At last he got vertical and said, "The seven continents. North America, South America . . . Holy smokes! Miss Simpson, look!"

"Holy smokes ain't a continent, Jughead!" Lucas taunted.

But Miss Simpson paid Lucas no attention. She followed my brother's gaze, and the color drained from her face. We all stopped talking and rushed to the window.

It was just after noon, but the sky had turned black as night. Dark green clouds boiled up on the horizon. Wind howled through the open window, and the whole building shook.

"Tornado!" Lucas yelled. "We're all going to die!"

A couple of the younger girls screamed. The Taylor twins started to cry.

"Quiet, all of you!" Miss Simpson ordered. "It's not a tornado. At least not yet. And no one is going to die."

She shut the window. "Since our school has no storm cellar, I believe we'd all be safer at home. If we hurry, we can get there before the storm hits."

"I rode my mare today, Miss Simpson," Lucas said. "I could take the twins home."

"Excellent. Mary Fay, Alice Ray, get your things and go with Lucas. Now."

The girls scrambled for their books and coats. Lucas led them out the door.

Miss Simpson said, "Those of you who live too far to walk home will come with me to my house. The rest of you go. Now. And hurry!"

We all went outside. The wind-whipped rain stung our faces and stirred up great clouds of dust. "Run!" Miss Simpson yelled.

Jess grabbed my hand and we sprinted

across the meadow, across the road that led
to town. The rain beat down, plastering our
hair to our heads. Mud from the newly
plowed fields sucked at our shoes. Jagged
lightning split the sky.

By the time we came in sight of the farm,
we were both panting and soaked to the skin.

"Thank goodness you're home!" Mrs.
Ravenell said when we burst through the
door. "Get some dry clothes and go to the
cellar."

"Jess? Caroline? Are you all right?" Pa
called.

"We're fine, Pa." Jess grabbed a handful of
candles and a tin of matches and ran out the
door.

"I'll need your help getting your father
down the steps and into the cellar," Mrs.
Ravenell said. "He won't be able to use his
crutches. Can you manage?"

"Yes, ma'am."

"Good. Let's go."

With Pa between us, we went out the door and started across the barnyard to the cellar. The rain came down in buckets, the wind tore our voices from our throats. Pa's face contorted with pain when we started down the steep cellar steps. By the time we got inside, his face was the color of ashes and his breath came in short gasps. We were all three winded and soaked to the skin.

"Are you all right, Pa?" I put my hand on his forehead.

"I'll be fine, sweetheart. That trip just took it out of me, is all." He closed his eyes and leaned his head against the earthen wall.

Above us, the wind howled. The cellar door slammed shut, plunging us into total darkness. Clods of dirt rained down.

"Jess," Mrs. Ravenell called, "where are those candles?"

Panic seized me. "Where *is* Jess? I didn't see him when we came down here."

"Jess?" Pa called.

The wind howled.

"Come on now, son. Stop playing around and light those candles. This is no time for hide-and-seek."

I felt sick. "He's not here," I said. "I'm sure of it."

"Then where is he?" Mrs. Ravenell demanded. "I saw him take the candles and matches. We both did."

"I don't know. Maybe he got hurt somewhere between here and the house."

"No," Pa said. "We'd have seen him. Something else has happened."

"Maybe he went back to the house for something," I said. "I'm going to go look for him."

"Don't be absurd, Caroline," Mrs. Ravenell said. "You can't go out in this."

"Well, I can't leave Jess out there alone. And Pa sure can't go looking for him."

"Then I'm coming with you," Mrs. Ravenell decided. "Will you be all right alone, James?"

Pa said, "I'll be fine. Just find Jess and get back here. All of you."

I felt in the darkness for the steps and climbed up. Mrs. Ravenell came behind me. It took both of us to push open the heavy cellar door. Rain and wind rushed in. We climbed out and closed the door and ran toward the house. The wind whipped our wet skirts and tore the pins from Mrs. Ravenell's hair. One of my shoes came off.

"Jess!" I yelled the minute we hit the house. "Jess! Where are you?"

"He's not here!" Mrs. Ravenell said. "He must be in the barn."

"You check there, I'll look in the toolshed."

Mrs. Ravenell shook her head. "No. I think we should stick together."

We plunged back into the storm, calling for Jess. In the toolshed, the shovel we'd used to make his hideout stood against the wall, dried mud still caked on the handle. It was then that I knew where he'd gone.

"The hideout! That's where Jess is!" I shouted.

"What? Why on earth would he—"

"I don't know why. I just know that's where he is. We have to go get him."

We ran for the field. When I looked back, I saw the funnel cloud gathering in the sky, spiraling toward the ground.

"Quick!" I yelled. "We have to hurry!" I held the fence while my grandmother climbed through. We ran along the creek bank, yelling for Jess. But the wind sucked out our voices and threw them away.

I splashed across the icy water to the cave. It was empty. I cupped my hand to my mouth. "Jess! Answer me! Where are you?"

Wind tore through the trees, bending them double. I stood on top of the cave, straining my eyes against the beating rain.

"There!" Mrs. Ravenell yelled, pointing through the trees. "There he is!"

I started running toward him, but she caught my arm and pushed me inside the cave. "Stay here, Caroline. I'll get him."

"But I can run faster!" I said. "I'll go."

"Don't argue, girl! Can't you see that tornado is practically on top of us?" She tore across the open field, waving her arms at Jess. Sonny bounded alongside Jess, seemingly unaware of the storm.

I huddled at the mouth of the cave, peering through the driving rain. It seemed forever before I saw three shapes coming toward me. Mrs. Ravenell pushed Jess and Sonny inside and squeezed in between us.

"The tornado is on the ground!" she yelled. "We'll have to wait it out here."

Sonny whimpered and licked my hand. The inside of the cave smelled like dirt and sweat and wet dog.

"Are we going to die, Caroline?" Jess asked, his voice shaking.

"Of course not," I said. "We made this cave really strong, didn't we?"

Jess nodded. "I . . ."

The rest of his sentence was lost in a great roar as the tornado swept over us. We huddled together, our arms wound around each other. Bits of roof, pieces of tin, fence posts, and uprooted trees flew past the opening to our cave. The whole earth groaned and shook.

Then it was over. The wind died. The rain turned to a light drizzle. I looked at Jess. His eyes seemed to take up his whole face.

"Are you all right?" I asked.

"I guess so." He patted our grandmother's shoulder. "Are you all right, Mrs. Ravenell?"

She swallowed hard. "I'm quite all right, Jess, no thanks to you. Why didn't you go to the cellar as you were told?"

"I started to, but I couldn't find Sonny."

He looked up at me. "I couldn't just leave him out there to die, could I?"

"I know you love Sonny," I said. "But you could have been killed, Jess. Pa is worried sick. We left him alone in the cellar to come looking for you."

"I'm sorry." Jess buried his head on my shoulder. "I was so scared when I heard the tornado coming."

"So was I," Mrs. Ravenell said.

Jess's head jerked up. "You? Pa says you're not scared of the devil himself."

"Jess!" I said, horrified.

To my surprise, Mrs. Ravenell burst out laughing. "Oh, he does, does he?"

Jess said, "Am I in trouble again?"

"That's between you and your pa." Mrs. Ravenell stuck her head out of the cave and looked around. "All clear. Let's get out of here and go get him out of the cellar."

We started home. Sonny bounded over the ruined fields, sniffing tree trunks and fence posts. Jess plodded alongside me, his head down.

"I'm sorry I caused so much trouble, Caroline," he said.

"I know. But you've got to learn to use your head, Jess. You could have gotten us all killed."

We came to what was left of our fence. We crossed it and ran for the cellar. Mrs. Ravenell and I pulled open the door and she shouted down. "James! Are you all right?"

"Fine!" Pa yelled. "Where's Jess? Did you find Jess?"

Jess bent down and stuck his face in the open doorway. "I'm all right, Pa."

Mrs. Ravenell and I climbed down and helped Pa up the stairs. We made our way across the muddy barnyard to the house. Our weather vane lay twisted in the mud, along with one of our sheep. Hay lay scattered everywhere. Part of the barn roof had blown into the field across the road. But the house was safe, and the windmill still stood spinning in the wind.

"Thank the Lord for that," Pa said. "And thank you, Abigail, for watching out for my children."

Mrs. Ravenell raked her tangled hair out of her eyes. "You're welcome," she said.

Chapter Six

We spent the rest of the week putting our farm back together. Jess and I straightened the toolshed, nailed the fence back onto its posts, and chopped the uprooted trees into firewood. Mr. McGuffey brought the rest of our neighbors to help put the roof back on the barn. Everything started to look normal again. Except the crops. Water stood ankle deep in the fields. The neat rows we'd spent a whole day planting were now a sea of mud. All that work for nothing.

Mr. McGuffey said, "I figured we were in for a stormy spring. I just didn't plan on it being this bad." He put a hand on Pa's shoulder. "Don't worry, James. Soon as it dries out, we'll plant again."

The next day, Miss Simpson rode her mare out to the farm to tell me that the Founder's Day program would go on as planned, even though the school had lost its windows and half the roof. In all the excitement of the tornado, I'd forgotten all about Founder's Day. Now I worried about having to recite my poem in front of the whole town.

Mrs. Ravenell said, "Don't be ridiculous, Caroline. Surely a girl who can manage a farm and ride out tornadoes can face a few of her friends and neighbors and recite a simple poem."

"But what if I forget?" I stepped out of the

green dress and handed it to her. Except for putting in a new hem, it was finished.

"You won't," she declared. "I have every confidence in you. When it comes to facing up to things, we Ravenells are a strong bunch. Your mother was a Ravenell, after all. I have a feeling you've inherited her spunk."

We Ravenells. It was the first thing my grandmother had ever said that made me feel we were even from the same planet. My heart swelled with sheer gratitude. My throat closed up and I swallowed hard. But I knew better than to let her see me cry. "I'd better go help Jess feed the sheep," I said.

"In a minute." She opened a velvet pouch and took out a gold heart on a chain. "This was your mother's. It's time you should have it."

She dropped it into my palm. It felt cool and solid in my hand. For a moment, I just stared at it. The feelings inside me were all mixed up and too deep for tears. There was so much I wanted to know about my mother. But whatever was happening between my grandmother and me was too fragile for words. This was not the time for questions. Maybe someday, but not yet. I remembered Mrs. Ravenell's telling me not to gush, so at last I said, "Thank you very much."

She nodded and the spell was broken. "You're welcome. Now, get dressed and go help Jess. I need wood and water."

On Founder's Day, two lambs were born. Jess and I found them near the pens when we went out to tend the sheep. They wobbled about on their little matchstick legs, bleating for their mothers. We waited to be sure their mothers would let them nurse, and then we went to find Pa.

His leg was much stronger, and the bruises on his face had finally faded. Sitting on the ground in the spring sunshine, making a new ax handle, he looked almost himself again. "Well now," he said to me, "are you ready to recite your poem?"

"I hope so. I hope I don't let you down."

"You could never do that, honey. Not ever. Not after all you've been through this year."

"Thanks, Pa." I bent down and kissed his cheek. He smelled like soap and wood shavings.

Jess said, "Pa, do you think Mrs. Ravenell might stay here with us if we asked her?"

Pa stopped working and squinted up at us. "What? Is this the same boy who hid under the porch and vowed not to come out till she left?"

Jess shrugged. "I guess I've got used to having her around."

"Me too," Pa said. "But it wouldn't be fair to ask her to stay on here. After all, she has a home in Charleston. All her friends are there. So, come next Saturday, back she goes."

He picked up the ax and fitted the new handle onto it. "And I want you to promise me you won't say one word to her about staying on here. We made a bargain and we'll keep it. Understand?"

"Yes, Pa."

"Good. Now help me up. It's time to get ready for the picnic."

When we got to the house, Mrs. Ravenell had our picnic packed.

Jess lifted the cloth on the basket. "Oh boy, fried chicken! Can I have a piece?"

Mrs. Ravenell said, "At ten in the morning? Certainly not! Hurry up now, Jess. Go change your clothes. And brush your hair. It's sticking up like a rooster's comb!"

Jess folded his hands into his armpits and flapped his elbows. "Bock-bock-bock!" He stalked across the floor, moving his head in and out in time with his jerky little steps. "Bock-bock-bock!"

Mrs. Ravenell rolled her eyes and shook her head. To me she said, "Come into my room. I'll help you dress."

The green dress and its matching jacket lay across the bed. She held it while I stepped into the long, sweeping skirt. Then she did up the row of tiny pearl buttons in the back. It was a perfect fit.

She gathered my hair into a loose braid and fastened the end with a silver barrette. Then she handed me the jacket and, finally, my mother's gold locket.

I looked at my reflection in her hand mirror. I hardly recognized myself.

"You look exactly like your mother when she was thirteen," Mrs. Ravenell said. "I can't believe I didn't see the resemblance before. You look quite beautiful, Caroline."

Pa knocked on the door. "Are you two going to spend all day in there?"

Mrs. Ravenell picked up her gloves. "Coming, James!"

Pa and Jess were waiting in the wagon when we came out. Pa gave a low whistle when he saw me. I felt my face turn hot, and I tried not to blush. But I couldn't help it.

"Quick, Jess. Go fetch me a fence post!" Pa said. "I'll need it to keep all the young men away from your sister."

"Oh, Pa!" Jess giggled.

"Isn't she lovely?" Mrs. Ravenell said, climbing onto the wagon seat. "So like Rebecca at that age."

Pa nodded. "I wish Rebecca were here to see this day."

"So do I."

Pa said quietly, "We could visit her grave if you like, Abigail. There's plenty of time."

Jess shot me a questioning look.

A meadowlark sang into the silence. Then Mrs. Ravenell said, "I don't think I—"

"I want to go, Pa," Jess said, his expression solemn. "I want to see Mama's grave."

Pa looked over at Mrs. Ravenell. She sat on the wagon seat, still as a statue. "I promised Jess I'd take him as soon as winter broke," he said. "We won't stay long."

I watched her shoulders sag as she let out her breath.

Pa picked up the reins. Jess gave me a hand up, and we clattered out of the yard and onto the dirt road.

Several days of hot spring sunshine had dried the mud into deep ruts. The wagon pitched and yawed its way toward town. Mrs. Ravenell clutched the wagon seat, her eyes on the ribbon of dirt road stretching before us. Soon, we turned off the road and followed a rutted lane to the top of a gentle bluff.

Jess and I helped Pa off the wagon and handed him his crutches. He swung around to the other side and held out his hand to Mrs. Ravenell.

She shook her head. "I'll wait here."

Jess opened his mouth to say something, but Pa stopped him with a look. He nodded to our grandmother. "We won't be long."

We walked along the rise to the grove of poplar trees shading Mama's grave. Jess slipped his hand into mine, and we stood looking down at the mound of brown earth. Pa cleared his throat. Then, bracing himself on his crutches, he leaned down and straightened the wooden cross he'd carved when Mama died, tamping it back into place with the toe of his boot.

The wildflowers Jess and I had brought last summer had died and blown away, leaving a handful of brown stalks in the dirt-filmed glass beneath the cross. Pa pulled them out and tossed them away.

Above us, the leaves of the poplar trees rustled in the wind, and the spring sunshine streamed in, dappling the ground. I heard a sound behind us and turned around.

Mrs. Ravenell came toward us, one hand

holding her hat in place against the breeze. We moved to make a place for her beside Mama's grave. She stared at it for a long time. Then she said, more to herself than to us, "Oh, Rebecca."

Jess kicked at the dirt, his head down. Tears spiked his dark lashes. His hand in mine felt small and hot. Suddenly, he wheeled and ran away from us through the grass, his arms and legs churning against the wind.

"Jess!" Pa yelled.

Mrs. Ravenell put her hand on Pa's arm. "Let him go, James."

The three of us stood in the lemon-bright sunshine, listening to the rustling of the trees and the humming of insects in the new grass. Mrs. Ravenell stood with her head down, her gloved hands clasped in front of her. Pa shifted on his crutches and draped his arm across my shoulders.

After a while, she lifted her head. "I never

was able to tame her, either," she said softly. "Parties, concerts, beautiful clothes—none of that ever mattered to her."

Her shoulders moved up and down in a tiny shrug. "She was happiest out walking the fields, or riding that old mare of hers. Said she liked the wide-open spaces."

She looked past Pa and me to the endless blue of the Dakota horizon, to the silver-green grasses waving in the wind, and the strip of dirt road curving into the distance. "I can see how she'd be drawn to a place like this."

Pa shaded his eyes with one hand. "She loved the land, Abigail. After a while it became as much a part of her as Jess is, or Caroline."

Mrs. Ravenell nodded, and Pa went on. "She was happy here. Clear up until the very end."

"Yes, I know that from her letters. Infrequent as they were."

The wind blew a strand of hair across her face. She tucked it back under her hat. "After the war, she was all I had. Then she came here to live."

She looked at Pa and me, her black eyes glittering. "I missed her so."

"You could have visited anytime," Pa told her. "You'd have been welcome here."

"I know that, James." She fumbled in her pocket for a handkerchief and dabbed at her eyes. "It was terribly selfish of me, I know, but I half hoped Rebecca would get homesick and come back to Charleston. When she didn't, it was easier to blame you, and the children, than to accept the truth."

Her shoulders sagged, and she gave me a small, sad smile. "Despite my best efforts, your mother chose a life completely different from the one I planned for her."

I didn't know what to say. Standing there in the wind-ruffled grass, with the hot sun on her shoulders, she looked completely defenseless and as fragile as old china.

After a moment, Pa said quietly, "It was a good life."

A yellow-throated thrush swept into the trees above us, her song rising, then fading into the stillness. Mrs. Ravenell took a deep, shuddering breath. "Well, we'd best be going. It won't do to make Caroline late for her program."

She took one last look at Mama's grave, then said to me, "Help your father back to the wagon. I'll get Jess."

We went back down the lane to the wagon. I helped Pa climb onto the seat, and we stowed his crutches. The horses tossed their heads and stamped impatiently, jingling their harness, and Pa said softly, "Whoa, there."

Then Jess and Mrs. Ravenell came up over the rise, holding hands, not speaking. At least not with words. Jess trotted along beside her, his eyes on her face. And suddenly her mouth curved upward in a smile so sweetly familiar that it made my chest hurt.

I glanced up, and saw that Pa saw it, too. For a moment, it was as if Mama herself were walking with Jess down the sunlit hillside.

They reached the wagon. There was no sound except the snuffling of the horses and the whisper of my grandmother's skirts on the grass.

She climbed onto the wagon and folded her hands in her lap. Jess scooted onto the seat beside me, but he looked past my shoulder to the little stand of trees marking Mama's grave.

No one spoke. The air around us felt charged, like it does just before a storm. Somehow, in the space of a single morning, everything had changed.

We all felt it. But it was a feeling none of us could put into words.

Pa flicked the reins. The wagon creaked. We went on toward town.

Chapter Seven

When we reached the picnic grounds, Jess
ran off to find Lucas, and I went to find
Miss Simpson and the others taking part in
the program. Pa and Mrs. Ravenell took
seats right down front with the McGuffeys
and the Taylors. The program began. I
was too nervous to pay much attention to
the others. I kept going over and over my

poem inside my head, hoping I wouldn't mess up in front of Pa and my grandmother, hoping my face wouldn't turn as red as a ripe tomato.

". . . reciting her original poem entitled 'Dakota Spring.' "

"That's you, Caroline!" Alice Ray Taylor whispered, and she shoved me onto the platform.

My heart hammered in my chest. I took a deep breath and looked at the sea of faces below. Mrs. Ravenell smiled and nodded. Pa winked at me.

"Dakota Spring," I began.

My heart seemed to have wings. I didn't worry about forgetting. I stood there in my grandmother's green dress and my mother's locket, and felt the strength of the Ravenells, and Pa's love coursing through me. My words poured out, easy as sunshine over a spring meadow.

When I finished, everyone clapped and

clapped. Lucas and Jess put their fingers in their mouths and made loud whistles. I looked down. Mrs. Ravenell dabbed at her eyes with her lace handkerchief. Pa's eyes glistened. I looked away. It was the first time I'd ever seen him cry.

After the program, everyone ate lunch beneath the trees or in the shade of the wagons. The younger children played tag in the meadow. The men tossed horseshoes. Even Pa threw a few, leaning awkwardly against his crutches. Jess and Lucas tied a rope to the branch of an old tree and took turns seeing who could swing the farthest. Miss Simpson brought out her guitar, and we sang "My Lady Love" and "Rowing on the Stanton" and "Hay in the Meadow."

At last, the shadows grew long. People gathered their children, their picnic baskets, their blankets and started home. Pa whistled for Jess. I helped Mrs. Ravenell pack our things. Jess and I hitched the team to the wagon and we started home through the gathering dusk.

The wagon creaked along the rutted road. The last rays of pink-tinged sunshine slanted through the trees. Frogs sang in the creek, and whippoorwills called from the tops of the cottonwoods. Jess fell asleep, leaning against Mrs. Ravenell. She drew him closer to her and wrapped him in our blanket.

"Whoa!" Pa finally said. We clattered to a stop in the yard. Sonny came out, barking and leaping up to lick Jess's hand.

Jess came awake. "Are we home?"

"Yes, son. We're here."

Jess yawned and said, "I had a good time at the picnic. Didn't you, Mrs. Ravenell?"

"I had a fine time, Jess." Mrs. Ravenell took a deep breath and looked up at the night sky. "Will you look at that."

Above us, the evening star shimmered, luminous and pure white. "You know, strange as it may seem, I shall miss this when I go back to Charleston," she said.

Jess blurted, "You don't have to go back. You can stay here with us! For as long as you want!"

She laughed, a soft musical laugh that lingered on the night air. "Why, thank you, Jess. That's the most attractive invitation I've had in a long time. I really must go home. But I tell you what."

"What?"

"I'd be most pleased if your father would send you both to visit me in Charleston next summer. Or better yet, he can bring you himself."

"Oh, Mrs. Ravenell," I said. "Do you mean it?"

"Well of course I mean it. Nothing would please me more. Except . . ."

"Except what?" Jess asked.

"Do you suppose you two could call me Grandmother Abigail?"

I started to cry. I couldn't help it. We sat there together, the four of us, beneath a night sky shot through with silver stars. And it was perfect, and that was all there was to know about it.